Captain Flinn
and the
Pirate Dinosaurs
The Magic Cutlass

Written by Giles Andreae

Illustrated by Russell Ayto

D0784136

For Rex ~ G.A.
To my brother ~ R.A.

PUFFIN BOOKS Published by the Penguin Group: London, New York, Australia, Canada, India, Ireland, New Zealand and South Africa. Penguin Books Ltd. Registered Offices: 80 Strand, London WC2R 0RL, England puffinbooks.com First published 2009. Text copyright © Giles Andreae, 2004. Illustrations copyright © Russell Ayto, 2004. All rights reserved. The moral right of the author and illustrator has been asserted. Printed in China. ISBN: 9780141501314

011

It was the day of Flinn's school play.
Flinn was a Pirate Captain (Flinn LOVES pirates)
and his friends Pearl, Tom and Violet were the crew.

"Go on," said Miss Pie,
their teacher.
"It's your song now."

"*I'm a pirate king
with a pirate ship.
And an ugly pirate crew,*"
began Flinn . . .

when another voice boomed out,

"And if you don't all come with me I'll eat the lot of you!"

"My goodness, he looks scary," whispered one of the parents. "Do you think he's a new teacher or something?"

The scary
pirate with the
booming voice was
enormous.

He had a big red coat,
huge black boots and
very scaly green legs.

He grabbed Flinn and his friends and disappeared off the stage.
"**no! no!** That wasn't meant to happen," shrieked Miss Pie.
"**Come back! COME BACK!!!**"
But it was too late.

Uh-oh, thought Flinn. Here we go again!

The pirate threw a large blanket over Flinn and
his friends, and they felt themselves tumbling
down
through
the air
until . . .

They landed right
on the main deck of an
old-fashioned pirate ship.

When they looked around,
they saw to their horror
that the pirates on
this ship were not
just ORDINARY pirates.

No, they weren't
ORDINARY pirates at all.
They were . . .

...PIRATE DINOSAURS!

There was

a Pirate Diplodocus,   a Pirate Triceratops,   a Pirate Stegosaurus,   a Pirate Pterodactyl

and, of course, their old arch-enemy...

the Pirate Tyrannosaurus Rex!

"Captain T. Rex," said Flinn.
"We meet again."

"Tie them up!"
yelled the Tyrannosaurus Rex.
"But leave
this one to me.
How
delicious!
What a treat!
Blood and bones
and scallywag
meat!"

"Then why don't you just go and get it!" shouted Captain Flinn back.

The great big T. Rex looked shifty. "Because, um . . . I can't swim," he muttered.

"Well, don't think I'm going to get it for you!" said Captain Flinn.

"Oh, but I think you will," said the Tyrannosaurus Rex, getting out his bottle of ketchup. "Because I'm feeling hungry and your little friends over there are looking tasty. VERY tasty indeed!"

"OK," said Captain Flinn angrily. "Then I guess YOU win."

So Pirate T. Rex and his fearsome crew,

and Captain Flinn and his captured mates sailed to sea.

It wasn't long before they reached

the exact spot.   Then Captain Flinn dived down, down, down under

the sea, dodging sharks and giant octopuses

until, at last, he found the cutlass.

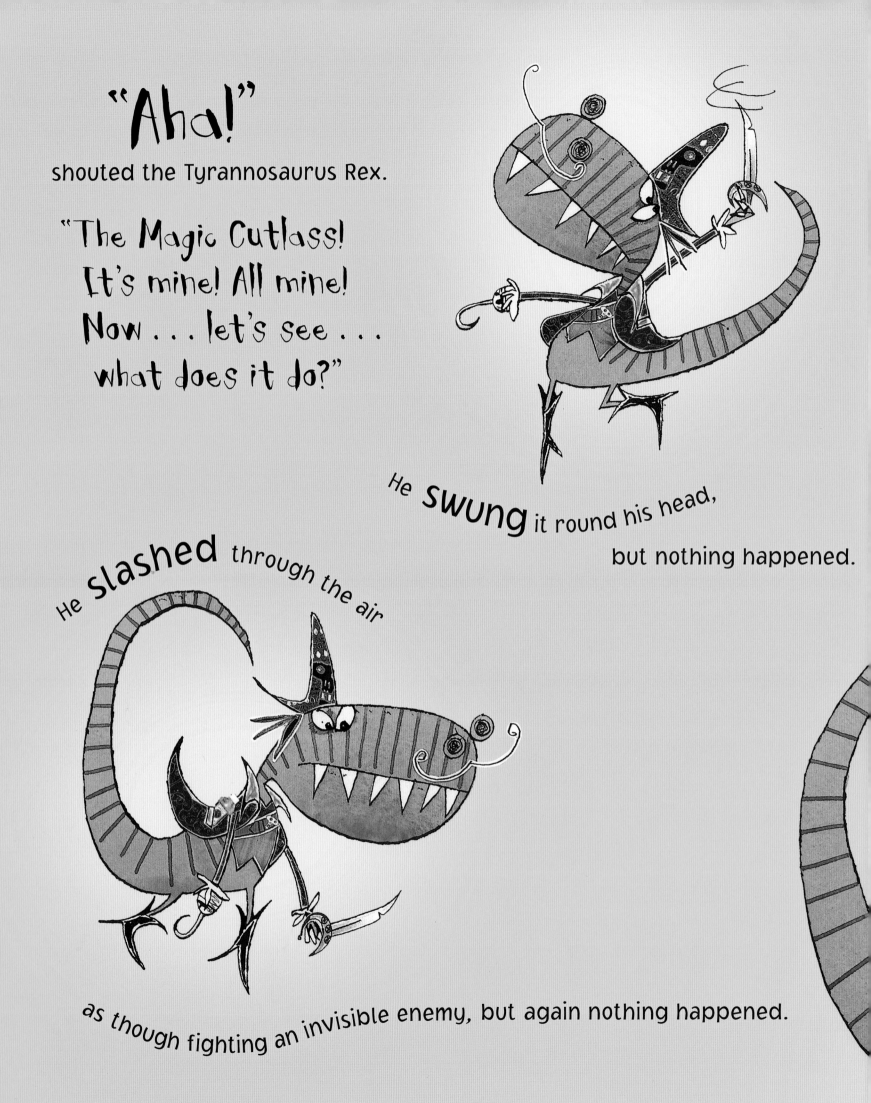

"Aha!"
shouted the Tyrannosaurus Rex.

"The Magic Cutlass!
It's mine! All mine!
Now . . . let's see . . .
what does it do?"

He swung it round his head,

but nothing happened.

He slashed through the air

as though fighting an invisible enemy, but again nothing happened.

He danced a jig and looked very silly,

but still nothing happened.

"Bother, blast and bellyache!"

roared the Tyrannosaurus Rex.

"This cutlass isn't magic at all. It's blunt and rusty and useless."

And he threw it away.

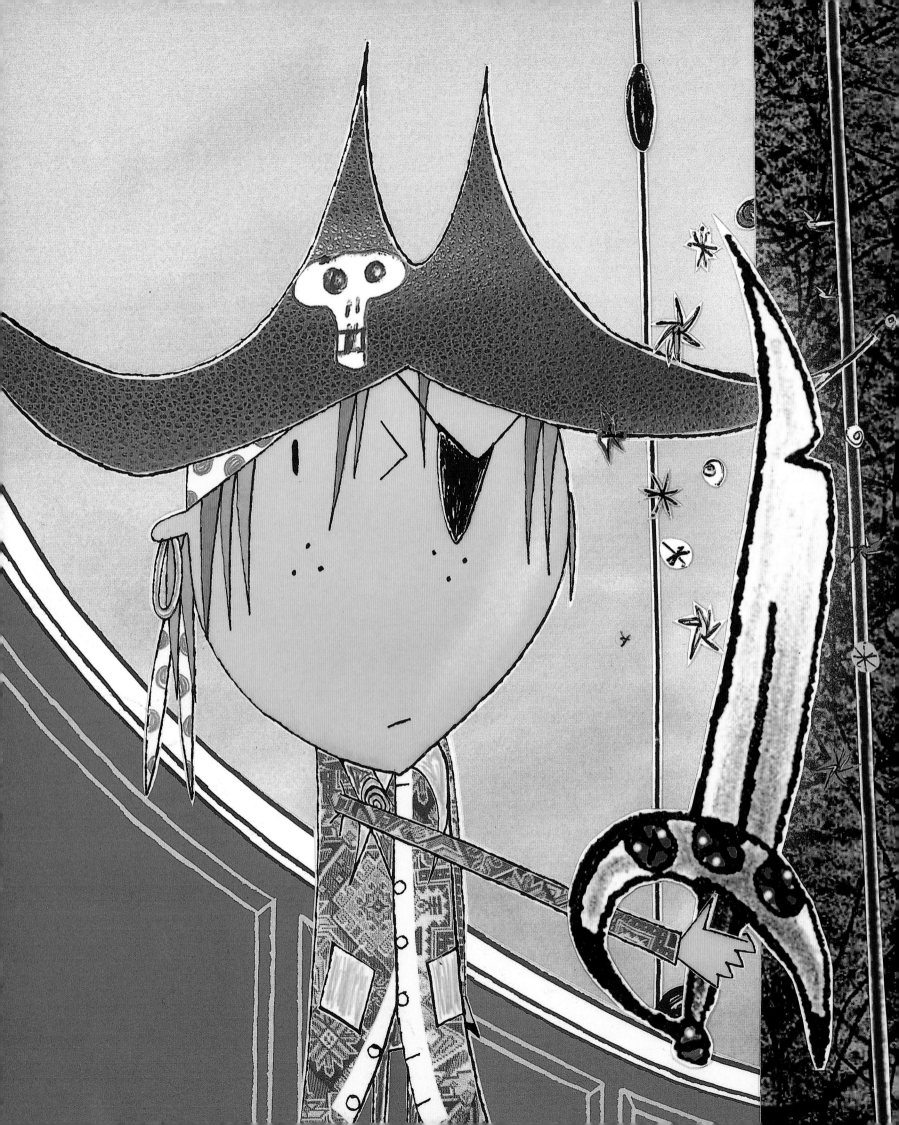

The cutlass
landed right beside
Flinn and he quickly picked it up.
"Oh, I wish I could untie these ropes," he said.

The cutlass began to *glow*
and suddenly the ropes round
Pearl, Tom and Violet fell
away
and his
friends
were free.

"That's it!" whispered Pirate Violet.
"That's the magic of the cutlass.
It grants wishes!"

Captain Flinn and his friends tried to sneak away,
but they were too late –
the Tyrannosaurus Rex
had spotted them.

"Not so fast!"

he roared,
snatching the cutlass back.

"I'm still hungry!"

"Well, you're not going to eat us, you great big fatso!" yelled Captain Flinn.

"Come on, gang – ATTACK!"

They swung from ropes and leapt from the rigging. Swords, cutlasses and daggers flew in every direction.

"Yo ho ho! Yo ho ho!" bellowed the Tyrannosaurus Rex.

SMASH!

CRASH!

The Pirate Dinosaurs were brave, but Captain Flinn and his crew were **even** braver and, after a long struggle, they finally had all the Pirate Dinosaurs safely tied up.

"Right-ho, matey," said Captain Flinn, marching the Tyrannosaurus Rex to the side of the ship. "Time to **walk the plank!**"

"But I can't swim!" shrieked the Tyrannosaurus Rex. His knees began to knock as he looked down and saw sharks circling beneath him.

"Help!" he yelled. "I want my mummy! Oh, I wish my mummy was here!"

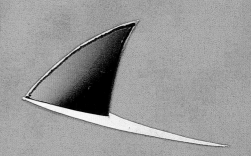

Suddenly, there was
a great
big
bang!
A huge **lady** Tyrannosaurus Rex appeared –
the cutlass had worked its magic AGAIN.

"Mummy??!!!!"

"What do you think you're doing?" bellowed the Mummy Tyrannosaurus Rex. "What did I say about only picking on people your own size? And how many times have I told you never to play with swords?"

"Um, sorry, Mummy," said the Tyrannosaurus Rex.

"What a naughty boy you are," said his mummy. "Now, give that cutlass back to the little boy and play together nicely!"

The Tyrannosaurus Rex grumpily handed the cutlass back to Captain Flinn. "Quick, gang," said Captain Flinn to his friends. "Hold on to the cutlass and say along with me, 'I wish we could go home!'"

The cutlass began to *glow*

and suddenly Captain Flinn, Pearl, Tom and Violet

found themselves flying through
the air until they

landed with a bump

back on the stage at school.

"Right," said Captain Flinn.
"Um, sorry about that.
Now, where was I? Oh yes . . .

I'm a pirate king with a pirate ship.
And an ugly pirate crew,"
began Flinn, when Miss Pie appeared.
"Where on earth have you been?"
she demanded. "And what's that sword
thingy in your hand, Flinn?"

But Flinn didn't answer. He decided to use the magic cutlass
and make one last wish. Miss Pie would probably never have
believed him anyway and actually she did look rather good . . .

. . . as a hippopotamus.